© 2012 Balivernes Éditions,
16, Rue de la Doulline, 69340 Francheville, France
Original title: La très grande carotte
by Satoe Tone
English language translation © 2013 Eerdmans Books for Young Readers

Published in 2013 by Eerdmans Books for Young Readers,
an imprint of Wm. B. Eerdmans Publishing Co.
2140 Oak Industrial Dr. NE
Grand Rapids, Michigan 49505
P.O. Box 163, Cambridge CB3 9PU U.K.

www.eerdmans.com/youngreaders

Manufactured at Tien Wah Press
in Malaysia in January 2013, first printing

19 18 17 16 15 14 13   9 8 7 6 5 4 3 2 1

Library of Congress Cataloging-in-Publication Data

Tone, Satoe, author, illustrator.
[Très grande carotte. English]
The very big carrot / written and illustrated by Satoe Tone.
    pages cm
Originally published in France in 2012 by Balivernes under the title:
La très grande carotte.
Summary: Six imaginative rabbits consider what they might make
from an unusually large carrot they have found.
ISBN 978-0-8028-5426-1 (alk. paper)
[1. Carrots — Fiction. 2. Rabbits — Fiction. 3. Imagination — Fiction.]
I. Title.
PZ7.T6162Ver 2013
[E] — dc23
2012048445

FSC
www.fsc.org
MIX
Paper from
responsible sources
FSC® C012700

The Very Big Carrot

Written and illustrated by
Satoe Tone

Eerdmans Books for Young Readers

Grand Rapids, Michigan · Cambridge, U.K.

One day, six rabbits found a very big carrot.
"Wow! What a very big carrot!" they said to each other.

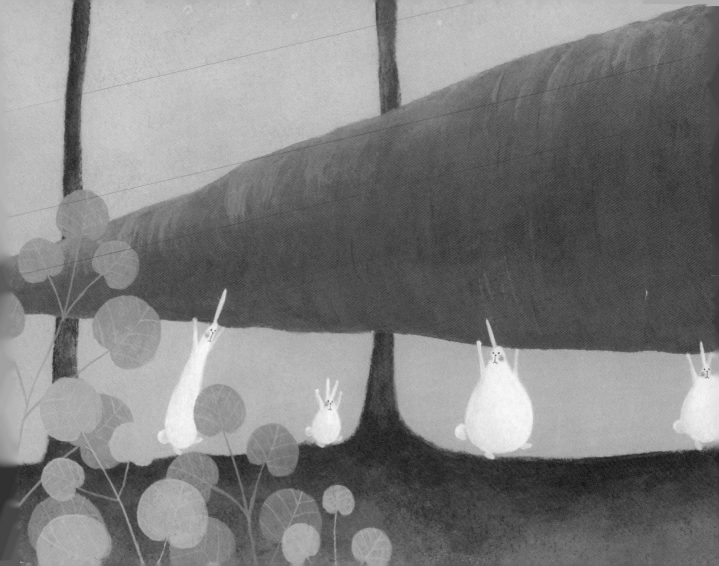

They dug up the very big carrot
and tried to think of the
very best way to use it.

What could they do with the very big carrot?
Maybe they could make it into a boat . . .

. . . and say hello to all the fishes!

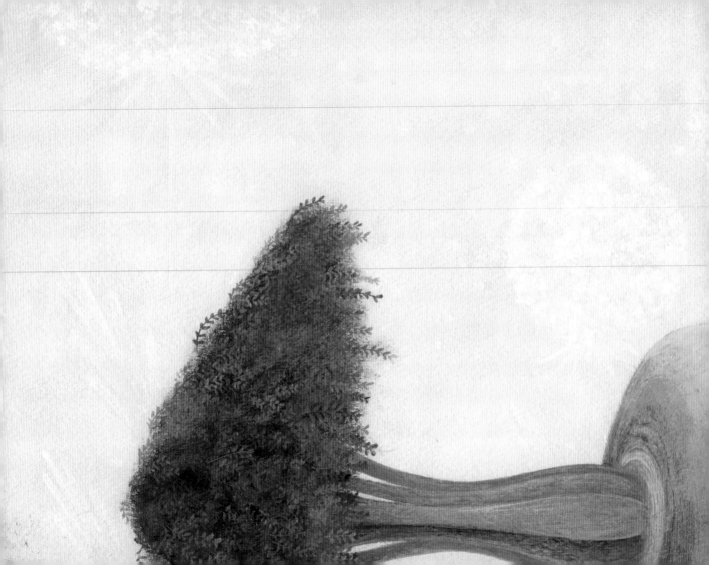

What else could they do with the very big carrot?
Maybe they could make it into an airplane . . .

. . . and fly away to far-off lands!

What else could they do with the very big carrot?
Maybe they could make it into a garden high up in the sky . . .

. . . and it would be the most beautiful garden ever!

What else could they do with the very big carrot?
Maybe they could make it into a house . . .

. . . and it would be the biggest house in the whole world!

Dreaming up so many things to do with the carrot
made all the rabbits very hungry.

But then they thought of one more thing
they could do with the very big carrot . . .

They could EAT the very big carrot!